The Search

I0556526

By: Olivia Hufford
Who May Or May Not Be Writing This Book
From The Limited Wifi
In The Backrooms

The Search
Copyright © 2022 by Olivia Hufford

ISBN 979-8-9866703-2-4

Printed in USA
Published by SIP Publications, LLC and Junior Authors
Designed by 5.13 Graphics & Media, LLC
www.thejuniorauthors.com

Dedication

This book is dedicated to all those who may
feel as if they're wandering their own
backrooms – sad, alone, confused, scared, even
angry.
Have hope. You will find an exit soon and see
the sun. I know you will.
And if you need the help of others along the
way?
Just reach out your hand. Call out. I'm sure
even in your backrooms, someone can find you.

On May 12, 2019, an anonymous user on 4chan began a thread asking people to post images that felt off. The anonymous user posted a picture of an empty office space, seeming to go on forever, with brown carpet, off - white walls and a generally lonely, creepy air to it.

A different user wrote a story explanation blurb that would go with it.

"If you're not careful and you noclip out of reality in the wrong areas, you'll end up in the Backrooms, where it's nothing but the stink of old moist carpet, the madness of mono-yellow, the endless background noise of fluorescent lights at maximum hum-buzz, and approximately six hundred million square miles of randomly segmented empty rooms to be trapped in. God save you if you hear something wandering around nearby, because it sure as hell has heard you."

And thus began the story of the Backrooms.

Sure, I am writing a story about the Backrooms.
Yet it is not the story.
That above blurb is "The" story of the backrooms. Whoever wrote it, and whoever first made the thread, thank you. You inspired my own take on this mythical, creepy place. If either of you are reading this, know that I thank you endlessly for helping inspire my imagination and write this story.

Now...how about I start?

1

The air was alive with the smell of autumn leaves and smoke. Leaves crunched under Sebastian's feet as he walked down the sidewalk to his best friend's house. A dog barked a few houses away. The wind rustled his black hair a little before dying down. The clouds parted for a moment, letting the warm sun kiss his arms before its shining face was covered again. It was a normal, quiet fall day.

Sebastian's phone dinged. A text from Chester, no doubt. He pulled out his phone and opened the message.

Ches: "Hey man. U there?"

"Yeah, cu in a few." He typed this reply quickly, hitting the send button. He wondered what had Chester so exited. He considered this as he stared into his black phone screen. His green eyes; startling, his mother had called them; stared back at him. His skin was milky white, his face framed with a mop of tousled black hair. Silently he asked his reflection if he knew what was going on.

Of course, his reflection didn't respond.

His friend had texted about ten minutes earlier, with lots of misspells and exclamation points. He said something about a breakthrough. Because his friend seemed so excited Sebastian promised to be there.

He finally reached Chester's house. It was the smallest one on the block, nestled at the end, at the cul – de – sac. White painted brick walls contrasted sharply with a dark red roof, with a slightly saggy porch at the front (It was solid enough for two people, at least.) He remembered that Chester's mother wanted to repair it, but when his father got sick the money had gone toward treatment.

He walked to the front door and rang the doorbell. After a moment Chester's mother, a petite Black woman of about 40 with piled, high braided hair, opened the door. She smiled as soon as she saw Sebastian. "Chester told me you might be stopping by."

"I'm sorry for the sudden appearance, Mrs. Spring." Sebastian said, a little sheepishly. "But yes, Chester did text me. He seemed very excited about something."

2

"He did seem out of breath when he came down to tell me that you'd be stopping by." Mrs. Spring stepped back. "Come in. He's been waiting."

"Thanks, Mrs. Spring." Sebastian gave her a grateful smile and headed upstairs. He was about halfway up when he heard footsteps and Chester appeared at the top, waving enthusiastically.

Chester was a tall, Black muscular teen. His dreadlocked hair hung down from his head, some of it dyed a bright pink for his support of cancer research. He wore a Cincinnati Red's T – Shirt and black running shorts. His eyes, always bright and full of energy, were a soft gray.

"Hey, Chester. What's up?" Sebastian smiled, coming to the top of the stairs. He greeted Chester with a high five, which was enthusiastically returned.

"Dude, you're not going to believe what I found." Chester's voice was breathless with excitement. "Come on, I'll show you!" He led Sebastian to his room, nearly pulling him along.

Chester's room looked neat, yet there were some messy parts. One corner of the room had his desk littered with papers and a few empty Pepsi cans. A few football posters decorated the wall, as well as a framed photo of him and his dad at the park before the sickness set in. His bed was neatly made, with a few clothes stacked on it.

Chester went to the desk and rifled around for a bit before coming up with a few papers. Old newspapers, by the looks of them. "Ok. Just bear with me here. Remember what I said about the place I was trying to find?"

Sebastian nearly facepalmed. Here we go again. "Chester...the Backrooms are not a real place."

"If they aren't real, then...explain this." Chester handed Sebastian the papers. Sebastian flipped through them. Every single one was about a missing person who disappeared, seemingly with no trace, near a warehouse on the southern end of town.

Sebastian frowned. "How does this prove that the Backrooms exists?"

3

"Because of the way these people disappeared. Look at this article." Chester pointed to the one Sebastian was currently holding. It was the story of some teen named Melody Bahrn.

"According to her mother, she had been talking on the phone with her when she was walking home, when all of a sudden she just...cut out." Chester began. "Completely. There wasn't even a dial tone. The location on her phone had been on but the last known location only showed the warehouse. When they had gotten there the phone wasn't there. No other traces of anyone else, either. But if the phone was gone, why was it still showing the warehouse as the last location? The location still seemed to be on."

Sebastian frowned again. "Chester, I really don't want to be a downer here, but... there could be a number of reasons why she disappeared. And not all of them include nice things." Sebastian sighed. "And the location thing...someone probably turned off her phone, which would save the last location as that warehouse."

"This happened multiple times. Not all of them were on the phone but all of them disappeared with just...no trace. Like they were just plucked off the street mid – stride." Chester shifted through the other articles. "Look. None of their belongings were found. DNA sweeps of the area turned up nothing. No signs of struggle. That doesn't just happen normally."

"Slow down, Chester. You have no idea what happened to those people. And there are horrible reasons someone disappears. Murderers. Kidnappers. Druggies" Sebastian shivered. "I don't want you running off and getting hurt."

"I'm not dumb, Seb. I'll take a knife."

"I know you aren't dumb. You're anything but. But I don't want you hurt." Sebastian cast his eyes down. "You're my best friend."

"I know I can be impulsive sometimes. But this may be the only lead I have. The events are too similar to be simple coincidences." Chester glanced at the picture of his dad on the wall. "And time is running out. My dad's cancer is getting worse, and my mom can barely afford the hospital as it is. Any

4

additional treatment might just send us over the edge financially."

"And what if it's not paranormal? What if we end up walking into a cult house?" Sebastian said.

"Like I said...I'm taking a knife. But I highly doubt it's a cult. There were never signs of a struggle in the areas they disappeared." Chester said, looking at Sebastian again. "Look, I know it sounds totally stupid and crazy, and...it could just be my desperation talking, but... something tells me there's more to these disappearances than just a crazy murderer or something."

"Let's say that the Backrooms are a real place." Sebastian said, sitting down on his bed. "How would you know where a cure for your father is?"

"That's the thing...I don't know if there's even a cure back there." Chester said sheepishly.

"So you're planning on walking into a paranormal dimension or whatever completely blind."

"Not blind." Chester shook his head. "I follow the Backrooms community on Reddit, and -"

At that comment Sebastian actually facepalmed. "Chester. You cannot believe everything you read on a social media site. Especially not Reddit."

"I know, I know, but...some of these stories tell of people suddenly just...finding themselves in the Backrooms. With no warning. Or they walked into a wall or touched a suspicious patch on it. People who were in our world and then just...not. Just like all these disappearances. Sudden."

"If they're in the Backrooms, then how do they have Wi - Fi?" Sebastian crossed his arms.

"...I don't fully understand how they have Wi - Fi, either." Chester admitted. "Maybe I'm reading too much into a glorified roleplay blog. But it's the only other way."

"Have you tried contacting the hospital? Friends, maybe, for financial support?"

Chester nodded, looking sad. "We've hit our credit limit for the hospital, and the only other contact my mom has is her sister... who absolutely refuses to help her. Something about my

5

mom learning how to live by herself and not 'leech off' of someone."

"That's horrible!" Sebastian gasped.

Chester shrugged. "Mom says her sister has always been like that. That that idea was a long shot, but she tried it anyway. She was that desperate."

"I'm still skeptical. Supernatural realms that people supposedly just appear in? Sounds kinda crazy..." Sebastian sighed and looked down. "Ches, don't get me wrong. You aren't crazy. And I'm not saying we should do nothing about your dad. But...maybe we can find a foundation or something that will help pay for your father's hospital room."

"We tried that. All of them are either nearly out of money or embroiled in various monetary scandals." Chester put a hand on Sebastian's shoulder. "Please, Seb. You've been my best friend for a long time. I know these Backrooms may not be real. We may just be poking around an old warehouse surrounded by coincidence after coincidence. But...I'm asking you to at least just...consider it for a moment."

Sebastian looked at his friend. Chester's gray eyes, a second ago excited and light, were now heavy with sadness and a little desperation. It was the look of someone who had met with closed doors at every turn, and now was grasping at any escape from the dire situation they were in. The eyes of someone who was so close to giving up yet wouldn't let themselves.

Sebastian nodded after a moment. "Alright… you've been there for me so many times. We can even go tonight, if you want."

Chester's face lit up. "Tonight? That sounds perfect! I'll tell my mom it's a late cuisine club meeting. I really don't like lying to her but… if we bring back a cure for my father it'll be worth it."

Sebastian smiled a little bit. "My folks are out of town, and they left me on my own because they think I'm mature enough to stay by myself. So, I'll be fine."

"Thanks, man. This really means a lot to me. Like...you listening to me rant about a possibly fictional place, even going

6

to help me check it out." Chester's eyes softened a little and he smiled.

"I know you'd do the same for me. Even if I was ranting about giant spiders in a cave or something." Sebastian smiled in response. "And spiders really creep you out."

"Maaaaaybe I wouldn't go if there were spiders." Chester laughed a little, taking his hand off Sebastian's shoulder. "But I'd end up going anyway, just because I'd feel guilty if I didn't."

Sebastian laughed at that. "Hey, I'd never force you to go."

Chester just mussed Sebastian's hair and Sebastian tried to duck, but didn't make it in time.

Talk then turned to other matters, of clubs and the weather, of video games and the math homework that they had promised each other they'd do that afternoon yet never got done. The sky outside turned from afternoon blue to gray dusk. Soon Chester and Sebastian said their goodbyes and parted, promising to meet at eleven o'clock that night by the outskirts of town.

Sebastian walked back to his apartment, humming some song that was floating at the back of his mind. He was mentally compiling a list of what to take – flashlight, maybe that metal crowbar in their garage, instant – developing camera that was sitting on top of his shelf....

His tune carried on the wind, as he walked home. Free as his thoughts.

And even though he was skeptical, there was a part of him that was so glad he got to have an adventure with his best friend.

\-

              \-

\-------

      \-

              \-------

interlude

—   —   —

—   —

—   — — — —

How would you describe nothingness?

It was a question often pondered in my time. Questions the scholars contemplated and the people asked the priests. Of course, even the priests didn't know, because who had experienced it?

Well, I can tell you the answer to that question.

It smells like musty air and slightly damp carpet. It tastes like dry air and rusty pennies. And it sounds like a never ending buzzing.

And it looks like an empty office building, with blinding fluorescent lights. And piles of things.

Most people assume when something goes missing, that it'll turn up eventually. Most of the time it does.

And sometimes… it gets lost permanently. And then it ends up here.

Nothingness.

There was another name for this place I heard during my short time on the plane of the mortals.

Purgatory. A place where the sinful dead go to repent their sins.

I never made up a purgatory. Never told my priests that there was one. Yet the human mind is imaginative and always trying to create new things where there once was a void.

For instance, giving me what they call a "gender."

In my time, you were either a "boy" or a "girl." I never understood that. Why humanity needed to be separated into "genders" was beyond me. For some reason they gave me a "boy" form. One with white skin and golden hair.

9

I can tell you that sometimes I felt like that. Yet sometimes I felt like I was one of those "girls." Sometimes I felt like I had a different hair color. Or a different skin color. Or I felt like I was skinless, hairless, and genderless... It was then I felt most at home.

I tried to tell my priests that my image should not be confined to one single form. That I looked like both the image they set forth and also the lady that stopped by the church every day with dark skin and braided hair, that I looked like the child with tawny skin clutching at her mother's hand, that I looked like the teenager with black hair and high cheekbones, that I looked like the youngest child and the oldest elder, that I looked like every race and every ethnicity and every gender... and yet my priests did not listen. Figures. Never let close minded humans paint a picture of you, especially if they must come up with one themselves. They will get it wrong.

I was a deity. I *am* a deity. Gender and race and ethnicity are things that do not bind me. I appear as I wish to people.

In this way, I can appeal to all. In this way, I can reach all. In this way, I can take care of all.

I wish others realized that I wasn't set in stone.

Maybe I wouldn't have ended up here.

I blame the priests, mostly. Like I said, trust humans to do anything and they will, I repeat, will screw it up. They're just too closed minded. They project their prejudices on you. They twist your image and force you to conform to what they believe is "right."

They put forth an image of me who was intolerant. I apparently said that loving the same gender was wrong, that wanting to be another gender was wrong. I apparently said that those with dark skin were lesser. I apparently said that "women" were lesser than "men" for no tangible reason.

Well, no wonder no one wanted to believe in me. I wouldn't have, either.

I went off on a tangent again, didn't I?

It's hard not to. I think back to my glory days, the days when people actually believed in me. Where people knew me.

10

Before the priests. Before the twisting. Before the decline of myself.

Now I don't even have a name. I'm reduced to a metallic, round, double – sided form lying on a pile of other lost things that ended up here by accident or on purpose. Oh, sure, I have some magic. But it's of no use to me anymore. No one is around to help activate it.

That's the thing about deities. Their power is only as great as the belief in them. And I can't remember the last time anyone truly believed in me.

I haven't ever found another deity. I wonder if there is any of those anymore. Other than me, of course. Just a forgotten deity lying on a pile of a forgotten items in a forgotten realm that most humans stumble upon by accident.

No one ever looks for the Nothingness. Or Purgatory. Or whatever you want to call it.

Sometimes I wish someone did. Just to help me out.

Sebastian brushed the hair out of his eyes, readjusting the backpack slung over his shoulder ans he looked around. He had caught the bus to this end of town. It was a bit of a walk, but he now stood on the gravel parking lot in front of the warehouse.

The warehouse...

It was a tall, foreboding building, boxy in shape. Its face was scribbled with graffiti, some faded, some fresh. Broken windows gave it the impression that it had multiple open mouths, all waiting to swallow its victims whole. One of the main doors was missing, and the other was gone completely. The hinges were rusty and the inside of the warehouse, as far as Sebastian could see, was as dark as night. Sebastian shivered and adjusted his backpack, which was full of the tools he needed.

A sound in the bushes caught his attention, and he whirled around. But it was just Chester, dressed in a hoodie and pants, both black. He had his own bag over his shoulder.

"Chester! You nearly gave me a heart attack." Sebastian said, breathing a sigh of relief. "Text me or something next time."

"Sorry, dude. I was just so excited." Chester looked up at the building. "So this is it, huh?"

"Yep." Sebastian said, looking up, at the tall building. It almost blended in against the near – midnight sky. "The place that could be the entrance to another realm."

"If this is the portal to another realm, maybe they should invest in a better welcome mat." Chester joked, laughing a little. Sebastian laughed along with him, before walking up to the front doors. "Well...this is it. Flashlights out."

Both boys rifled around in their backpacks, pulling out flashlights.

"Here we go..." Sebastian clicked on his flashlight and entered the building. Chester followed him with his own flashlight.

The circle of illumination the flashlight provided revealed a place that had been long abandoned. Motes of dust hung in the air. The flashlight beam traveled over steel beams that were half

12

covered by shredded tarps, piles of chains lying discarded on the floor, and termite – eaten palates lying haphazardly on the floor.

Chester shivered. "Geez...this place is creepy."

"You said it, dude," Sebastian replied, in a whisper. Why he whispered was a mystery to him, but somehow it felt right.

"Let's go from left to right. We can search that way." Chester led the way, leading them all the way to the back. Their footsteps echoed around them as they walked, sounding very loud in the abandoned atmosphere. Somehow, the boys were feeling as if they were disturbing a sacred spot.

They reached the back right corner of the warehouse and stopped.

Right in front of them was what looked like a runaway case of black mold. It was an ugly splotch on the wall of the warehouse. And if it wasn't black mold, it was the ugliest graffiti anyone had ever made. Even in the blackness of night, it seemed to out – dark the darkness. It was something you wanted to look away from yet couldn't take your eyes off of. And it was about the size of a large basketball, near the middle of the corner.

"...That thing doesn't look like it came from this dimension." Sebastian said, running his flashlight over it.

"It doesn't feel right, it makes me kinda uncomfortable... we must be on the right track!" Chester sounded scared but excited.

"Chester, be careful. We have no idea what that is. It could be black mold. Don't touch it until you know it's safe." Sebastian warned, holding his friend back.

Chester picked up a chunk of concrete lying near his shoes and threw it at the splotch on the wall. The rock hit the spot and clattered off the wall to the ground. No residue from mold or anything on it.

"See? It's safe." Chester walked up to it and hesitantly poked at the spot.

Nothing happened.

Sebastian came up and poked it with his flashlight. Still nothing happened.

"...that was disappointing." Chester said, after a moment. He looked almost crestfallen. "I guess...my imagination was acting up."

13

"It's ok, dude. I kinda saw it too." Sebastian said, turning away. "There's still the rest of the -"

He was suddenly jolted backward. Sebastian registered Chester yelling his name, before he hit the wall and his world turned black.

Meanwhile, Chester looked on horrified as his best friend was suddenly pulled back, by an unseen force. He had been talking to him one moment, turning away from the wall with the splotch, when he suddenly lurched backward, as if pulled by an invisible force. Chester tried to catch his hand, but it was too fast. Sebastian hit the wall, and....

Chester expected a wet crunch. What he didn't expect was for Sebastian to just...vanish. The flashlight and his bag fell to the ground, clattering.

Chester stood there, shocked into silence. What had just happened?

He went over to Sebastian's backpack, picking it up and looking it over. Then he looked at the flashlight. Nothing seemed off, so what -

His thought process was interrupted by the feeling of something suddenly yanking his head back. It felt like something was pulling his hair. He was pulled to the wall, and his world turned black before he hit it. His bag and flashlight clattered to the ground, next to Sebastian's.

All was quiet in the warehouse now. The wind whistled through the broken windows, but the sound was subdued. The chains hanging from the ceiling swayed slowly. All whispers of sound seemed to have faded.

And in the back corner, two bags sat, recently dropped. Two flashlights illuminated the dusty air, their beams aimed aimlessly at the wall.

The wall that no longer held a splotch.

interlude

...Someone is here.

I do not know how I know. All I know is that the air back here...it has changed. It feels heavier, somehow. It feels like...people.

Living people...it has been a while since someone has come back here. The last time someone came back here they didn't last very long. It was a few days, but they suffered. They screamed and cried and left behind only a journal full of nonsense. I caught names. The names of people they cared about, no doubt. Claire and Jenna.

That was a while ago. I don't know how long it has been. Time is strange here. Some days drip like molasses. Other days rush like a river. Time is fluid and has no meaning.

What has meaning, when you are forgotten?

But the air has grown...not musty. Heavy, but not dead anymore.

The dimension has found two others.

I do believe that I may yet have a way out. If they find me, that is. This dimension goes on forever, for there are many things that have been forgotten and have wound up here. As the world moves on and things move into the shadows, entire places, hollow and devoid of life, become part of this world.

And sometimes, when people wander into the wrong place at the wrong time, the dimension reacts instinctively. Forgotten or not, those people become part of this dimension.

Most simply die of insanity. But those who survive grow to become...things. Things that aren't human. Not anymore. They become twisted. Evil. Distorted.

And then there's Him.

He used to be a man. A man who was obsessed with this place. With the forgotten.

He shut himself away, from everyone and everything, lost in His research. He himself had been in the background most of his life, so it was easy for Him to disappear, to become one of the

16

forgotten. His parents had died, and He had no friends. No one remembered Him.

And so, the dimension found him.

He accepted that fate gladly, determined to find out everything about this place. He wandered this place, setting up His new research.

But as with everything else in this place, even the sane become twisted. It's only due to the fact that I am a deity that I have avoided that transformation.

He slowly lost his humanity. His desire to become forgotten and learn about this place slowly took away every single defining feature he had. His face. His features. Even His name. Now He is simply a shadow, a humanoid figure made of darkness. All I know about Him, is that He set out to conquer this place eventually. Now He can command the creatures like him – the humans who were forgotten. The ones that aren't humanoid at all.

But the dimension rebels against Him. He should not have this power over this dimension. Every chance it can it tries to swallow Him, to destroy Him outright. But He has a strong will. And so, He fights for control of this dimension. This war has been going on for a while.

Maybe that is why this dimension took these two. To save itself.

Whatever the reason I hope that these two do not fall prey to Him.

For it is a fate worse than death, to become part of his morbid menagerie.

Saturday, October 1?

The first thing Sebastian registered when he came to was the buzzing. It sounded like a nest of hornets above him.

He groaned and tried to sit up. His head hurt really badly. Dimly he realized Chester was lying next to him.

Sebastian finally blinked the clouds from his eyes and took in his surroundings.

He was in what appeared to be a hallway, in an office building. The floor was a light beige carpet, the walls a yellow that appeared faded and pocket marked.

And all around them, there was just...stuff.

Piles of small plastic toys, single socks, pieces of paper... a conglomeration of junk or things you might have kicked under your bed while cleaning your room and never pulled back out again just lay in piles around the hallway.

Chester stirred, and Sebastian looked that way. He helped his friend sit up.

"...Seb, what happened? Where are we?" Chester said, rubbing his eyes.

"...Chester, I don't think we're in the warehouse anymore." Sebastian said.

That made Chester look up, and look around. "...I don't believe it. We're actually... in the backrooms."

"Are you sure? Did the Backrooms have all this clutter, according to your sources?" Sebastian kicked at one of the piles half – heartedly.

"...no, but what other explanation is there? And this place looks similar. I'm starting to think that I was just reading too much into a role play blog." Chester stood up, looking around. "But wherever we are, it's not the warehouse."

"Well, let's assume this is the backrooms. What do we do now?" Sebastian said, looking around. The hallway continued before turning right on one end, and on the other end it opened into an empty room, with no piles of stuff.

"...We look for a cure, I guess." Chester poked at one of the piles. "Maybe there's something in here?"

"Why is all this stuff here anyway?" Sebastian asked. "I mean... how did it get here?"

18

"I don't know. Don't ask me." Chester shifted through the piles. "It's nothing but junk." Then his hand clinked against something. "Hey...except for this." He held up the object.

It was a coin, but it was unlike any coin they had seen. It was made out of a coppery substance, like a penny, but it was too big to be a penny. Almost the size of a quarter. And the designs were unlike anything they had seen. On one side there was a large tree, with a canopy of leaves that stretched from one side of the coin to the other, but not the other side. The trunk was thick and extended into several dozen roots, reaching the bottom of the coin. On the other side was the image of an ancient city, with an obelisk with a star on top in the center.

"...I've never seen anything like it." Sebastian said, reaching out and touching the coin. It felt cool and smooth.

Of course you haven't. I'm not supposed to be a coin, you know.

Sebastian jerked his hand away and Chester nearly dropped the coin. "Did that thing just...talk?"

You know I can still hear you. I'm not a thing, you know.

"...you can hear us? Who are you?"

I don't even remember my name. This place has that effect.

Sebastian and Chester looked at each other. "How are you talking...what are you?" The voice was ethereal, neither male nor female, and it echoed in their minds.

I was once a great deity, you know. I commanded armies of priests and had the world enthralled in my religion. Now... because in my arrogance I chose the wrong people to lead my religion on Earth... I am reduced to this, stuck in the place for forgotten things.

"The place for forgotten things? Is that what the Backrooms is?" Chester asked, looking around. It did make sense. The piles of stuff contained things easily forgotten. The scenery around them was an everyday, mundane, forgettable office space. It was the epitome of "forgotten."

If the "Backrooms" is what you call this place, then yes. But what you call this place does not matter. It is the place for the forgotten, for the parts of humanity that have faded into the shadows.

19

"...why did I ever want to come here?" Chester groaned. "Everyone has gotten it all wrong. This place isn't anywhere I can find a cure."

You were looking for this place? An unwise choice. And what do you mean by cure?

"...My father is very ill. He will die if I cannot find a cure."

The voice seemed to consider something for a moment. Then...

I might be able to help with that.

"Wait, really?" Chester said. Sebastian's eyes widened. "...You can save Ches' dad?"

I did not lie when I said I was a deity. Even with my limited power, your own belief in me had bolstered me enough to speak. If I may escape this place, perhaps I can help heal your father.

"...what's the cost, however?" Sebastian said. "Nothing on Earth comes totally free." He shot a warning glance at Chester. Chester realized what he was doing and raised his guard.

All I ask is that you get me out of here. I do not even care if you do not join my religion. If I get back to the world I will heal your father and try to start anew. This, I make my most solemn vow to you.

The coin heated up in Chester's hand.

"...Alright. That's...not impossible. We can do that." Chester smiled wide. "Five seconds in here and we've found a cure. Now...where's the exit."

Sebastian looked around. There was no visible exit from where they were.

Do you mean to tell me you came in here not realizing escape is nearly impossible?

"...Excuse me, what?" Sebastian addressed the coin.

The coin seemed to sigh. Chester stared at the coin in his palm in disbelief.

This "Backrooms" is not anything that any of you comprehend or understand. This place is a living dimension, swallowing and claiming all the forgotten places and things on Earth. It is infinite. And right now, it is hurting.

20

"...What do you mean, it's hurting?"

...Humans like you have wandered in here before. But it is not a pretty sight. They go insane and turn into monsters. But...there was someone who searched for this place obsessively. And He found it. But His obsession with the forgotten turned Him into one. And He commands all the fallen humans here – the monsters, the things that stalk the shadows. And the dimension doesn't like it. And so it has tried to recruit outside help. That was why you were able to find it so easily.

"...It let itself be found? Could this be the reason why...the others disappeared?" Sebastian said, looking around. "Was it taking people...to heal this hurt?"

Most likely, yes. But obviously...those people did not make it. I have felt the air in this place change. It used to be static...but with every fallen human He adds to His army the air grows more oppressive. This place is shifting and if it falls under His control...Earth is in danger of disappearing into forgetfulness forever.

"...But why is whoever He is, wanting to make the world forgotten?"

...perhaps He wishes for the world to be twisted the same way He was.

"...can we have a moment?" Chester said, setting the coin down on top of the pile. Then he pulled Sebastian aside.

Both boys just stared at each other for a moment.

"...are we both going crazy?" Chester whispered. "Even I have to admit...this supernatural stuff goes deeper than I thought."

"Like it or not, we're in this and we're in this deep." Sebastian sighed. "Or, any moment now, we'll wake up on the floor of the warehouse fresh from a mold – induced fever dream." He looked down and laughed a little. "Man...this is just crazy. We find an entire deity just sitting on top of a pile of junk, disguised as a coin. It starts speaking to us -

They.

"...you can still hear us?"

Yes, But I tuned you out to be respectful. I don't have enough energy to disassociate myself from you. But please, call me they.

"...fine, they start speaking to us, saying the Backrooms is a living dimension, that pulled us in because it needs help, and that they can cure your father, if you help us out. Meanwhile, there's an inter - dimensional war brewing because a crazy is loose in the Backrooms." Sebastian sighed. "I'm glad we found the deity...but should we help defeat this thing?"

"Maybe if we do, we can find a way out of here." Chester said. "If we help the Backrooms, maybe it'll help us by letting us out."

"...there may be something to that. The faster we defeat this...He, the faster we get out of here."

Chester nodded. "And the faster we can save my dad."

The boys walked over and Chester picked up the coin. "Alright. We'll get you out of here, but first we need to defeat this Mysterious He. If the Backrooms brought us here to defeat Him, then maybe it'll let us go when we do."

A wise plan. A word of warning, however – He excels at mind games. You must learn not to trust everything your eyes show you. Look with your heart, not with your eyes. And also... trust in one another, and me. If you doubt each other, He will use it against you.

"Alright. Now...how would we go about finding this Mysterious He?"

He wanders the Backrooms, but is drawn to the still sane and living. He knows you are here, most likely, and will send his monsters after you.

"Could we possibly save those who turned?"

...unfortunately, no. Even if you were able to retain their human forms their minds would never be the same. They are lost, forever, I am afraid.

"...how would we go about...y'know..."

Killing them is a merciful act now. They are no longer human. And anything will do the trick. Bashing their heads in is the only way to kill them. I'm sure there's something in this pile that can count as a weapon.

Sebastian and Chester shifted through the piles of debris lying around. Sebastian found a wooden board and Chester found a rusted pipe.

"...Now what?"

I suggest we move. Find a safe spot to make a camp. A base to rest in.

The boys began to move deeper into the Backrooms. It was kinda surreal, if they were being honest. The buzzing of the lights always stayed constant. The walls never changed, just sometimes were a slightly darker shade of yellow. The carpet slightly squished under their feet.

And the piles of stuff were still around. Some of it was different than the stuff they found originally. Sebastian traded out his wooden board for part of a steel pole.

Sometimes they would see the black patches, but it would disappear as they came closer to them.

They walked for a long time with no change.

Eventually the boys began to get tired. They had come here late at night, and they hadn't gotten sleep before this.

"...Maybe we should stop here." Sebastian yawned.

Chester nodded and looked around. "Hey, look. Over there. It's a doorway that leads to a dead end. Let's stay there."

They gladly trudged to the dead end, sitting down against the wall. Sebastian leaned his head back and closed his eyes.

If you are resting, you must be careful. If you hear something, run. Or at least, stay quiet. Many of the monsters cannot see well. But their hearing has evolved. So, whatever you do...be quiet.

"Got it." Chester yawned quietly, and curled up, head resting on the wall. Sebastian sat against itand stared at the slightly – water – stained ceiling.

"Dude, get some sleep. You look bushed." Chester said, quietly.

"...None of this rattles you even the least bit?" Sebastian asked his friend.

"At first, it was all kinda crazy...but if you think about it man...if this is real life, then what else are you supposed to do but just do your best with what the situation is right now? And if this a dream, then what's the harm in participating?" Chester

23

said, rolling on his back. "...I finally found one hope for my dad, no matter how far – fetched it is."

Sebastian went quiet at that. He wondered what it was like – knowing the one hope you had for your dying father was a deity from a coin that may or may not all just be a mold – induced dream, and you were lying passed out on the floor of an abandoned warehouse. And if it was real, you had to fight your way out of a crazy insane dimension that sucked you in here because a madman was trying to take over. So there was no guarantee that you'd be able to save your father.

It wasn't long before Chester had fallen asleep. But Sebastian stayed awake and just wondered.

24

I find feed I find feed I find feed

No, I am intelligent

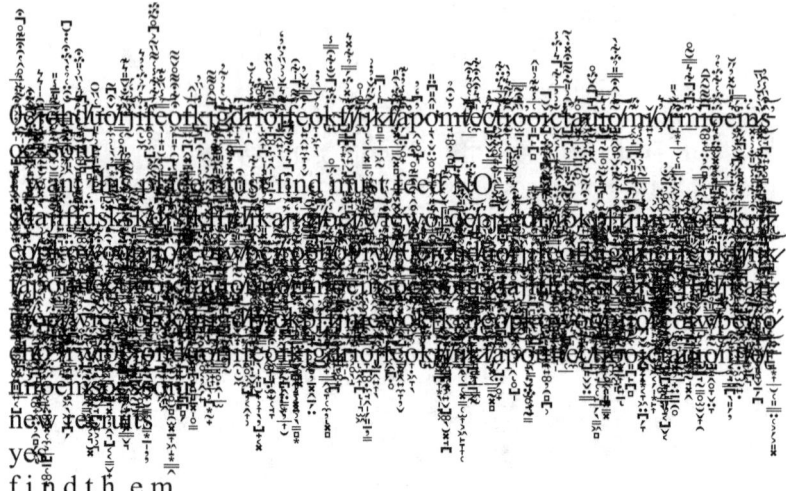

I want this order must find must feel NO

new recruits
yes
f i n d t h em

Backrooms Day 1

The first thing Sebastian noticed when he finally woke up was that Chester was already awake. He was apparently holding a silent conversation with the coin, staring at it intently.

"Chester? How long have you been up?" Sebastian yawned, sitting up.

"Oh! You're up." Chester startled, nearly dropping the coin.

"Sorry if I scared you, man." Sebastian said, stretching and sitting up.

"It's cool. Just don't do that again." Chester let out a laugh and smiled a little. "I've just been talking with the Deity."

Sebastian nodded. "That does sound cool." Sebastian said, stretching his legs in front of him. His legs ached from sleeping in a cramped position all night.

Morning. How do you feel?

Sebastian jumped, before sighing. "I will never get used to that."

I know having someone in your head can get some getting used to. Don't worry – I won't poke around where you don't want me.

"Thanks." Sebastian said, gratefully, before turning towards Chester. "Now. Where do we start?"

"I think we just have to...wander." Chester said. "If the Backrooms works the same way it does in stories...and if it really wants our help to defeat this mysterious He, it will lead us to where we need to go."

Sebastian laughed a little. "Dude, you sound like one of those cheesy wizards in your little cousin's stories." Sebastian hunched over, using his metal pole like a cane. "Now remember, great hero, you must follow your heart to complete this quest." He said in what he hoped was an old man voice.

Chester laughed, and so did Sebastian.

You humans are so strange.

When they recovered, they began their walking.

Once again, it was nothing but those walls, and that floor, and that maddening hum in the background. Their footsteps were soft on the carpet. There were no other sounds that they could hear.

Until...

A soft thumping.
Both boys froze.
Oh no...
"What is it?" Chester whispered, still frozen on the spot.
The thumping grew louder.
Whatever you boys do, don't move! I recognize that sound... all you need to do is stay totally silent. Because this thing is ⁻
It rounded the corner. And the thing that did would stay imprinted on the boy's memories for years and years to come.
It was a tall, skinny...creature. Its feet looked like hooves, if hooves were blobby and stuck to the floor like slime. Its hands seemed to be shifting, first with two fingers, then five, then three, and then back to two. It was entirely black, with white eyes that scanned the area. It had no mouth. It seemed to be made of some kind of black goo, but it left no trace behind. It was so tall it stretched to the ceiling and its head was twisted down to avoid it.
Sebastian and Chester were frozen with both fear and revulsion. The thing in front of them repulsed every single one of their senses. It was a perversion of humanity, something that should not exist in any dimension. Unnatural, even for this place. It was a monster in every sense of the world.
The thing looked around. It twisted its neck three – sixty degrees, accompanied by horrible cracking sounds. It took every ounce of self – control for the boys not to flinch or run screaming.
The coin was quiet. It had grown cold.
Could a deity be afraid? Perhaps.
The thing looked around, unblinking, with its unseeing eyes. What was it seeing? What do you see when you're blind?
The thing stretched out its arm and felt its way along the wall. Sebastian was frozen, standing so close to it as it moved its arm. He was trying not to break down. It was so wrong, and he didn't want it anywhere near him. This close he could feel the...negativity radiating off of this thing. What feeling it really radiated couldn't be placed in this day and age and Sebastian doubted it would ever. Negative seemed to be the best word for it.

It stopped only inches from the side of his head. The monster seemed to stare directly into his soul. Its breathing sounded like a labored rattle. Its white eyes seemed to pierce his soul and lay bare all the insecurities he ever had. Chester, watching this, was staring with wide eyes, and hoping that the thing didn't move a few feet to the left.

Finally, it moved its arm away. Turning, it seemed to survey the rest of the room with sightless eyes and then it slowly walked away, its thumping footsteps fading as it went back to who knows where.

It seemed like forever before the three of them relaxed. Chester let out a breath that he didn't know he had been holding in. Sebastian collapsed to the floor, his legs giving out. The coin grew warm again.

We have survived our first encounter with the Lost.

"The Lost?" Sebastian said, looking up from the floor. "Is that what they're called?"

Yes. The Lost. Those who have fallen to become part of His minions. They turn inhuman, so consumed by the black void of forgetfulness.

"…I…that was the most terrifying thing I had ever seen" Chester stuttered out, trying to help Sebastian back up. "I…don't know how to say it, it was just…"

Unnatural? Felt like it should not be there? Felt like looking at it, you could see it trying to mesh with a world that did not want to accept it?

"…yeah. Exactly." Chester said.

"In any case. We need to move. That was too close of a call to stay here." Sebastian said, picking up his metal rod. Chester picked up his pipe and nodded, and the two began to walk once again.

"You know…if this place is endless, how will we ever find this Mysterious He?"

I have found that here, the direction matters less than you think.

"Isn't that such a clear answer." Sebastian muttered sarcastically.

29

"He means as long as we want to find it, we will find it. I think." Chester said. "This place doesn't seem to have set places – they just appear and disappear as they please."

"That makes all of this sooo much easier." Sebastian said, rolling his eyes.

"We'll find a way out. We'll defeat Him. I know it." Chester tried to sound upbeat. But he was unsure.

The coin was quiet throughout the whole exchange.

They walked for a little while longer. But eventually, they noticed something.

"Is it just me, or is it...getting darker?" Sebastian said, looking up. Indeed it seemed the lights that populated the ceiling were increasingly dark or dead. "Yes...it does seem to be getting darker." Chester said, clutching his length of pipe. "Is it...Him?

No, It is not. It is simply the Backrooms, changing. For there are levels to this dimension, that you can pass through. As forgetfulness has levels.

"Weird...so this place can change." Chester said. "If I'm being honest, I thought it would just be..." He gestured to the walls and piles of forgotten things. "This, forever."

Some people do get stuck here. They are forever unable to change. Some just. . . fade. Others turn into monsters. Only those who are willing to keep going make it further.

"...What is this dimension, one big test?" Sebastian said, a little frustrated. "Levels of forgetfulness...getting stuck if you can't bear to move on...what does this place even mean?!"

I have found, The coin replied, That this place means nothing and everything. What that means is up to you.

Sebastian sighed. He hoped this wouldn't take much longer. The deity in this coin was beginning to annoy him due to their vagueness, and he wasn't sure how much longer he could bear watching yellow walls pass by.

interlude

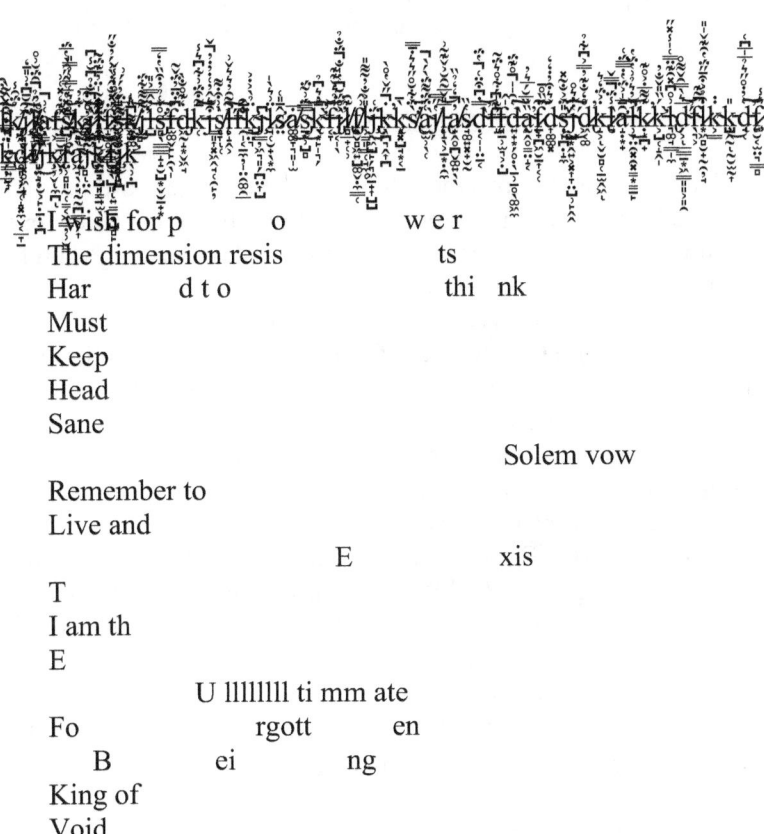

I wish for p   o   w e r
The dimension resis   ts
Har   d t o   thi nk
Must
Keep
Head
Sane

                   Solem vow
Remember to
Live and
            E   xis
T
I am th
E
       U llllllll ti mm ate
Fo   rgott   en
  B   ei   ng
King of
Void

Two threaten me
They must
 D
       I

               E

It was so dark.

That's what the boys thought as they moved forward.

The lights were flickering, their buzzing being cut short for a second before reactivating. Instead of a constant buzzing sound, it was a stuttering sound now.

Somehow it was even worse than the constant.

Sebastian and Chester were forced to keep their flashlight on. They didn't want to, for fear of getting discovered, but the darkness was scarier.

"How much longer do we need to go?" Sebastian asked. He had just woken up what felt like moments ago, and yet... this placed seemed to be draining him of energy fast.

"I don't know. But something's happening. And that's good. Maybe we can get out. It'll lead us out, I mean." Chester said.

"Maybe, yeah. Or maybe we'll get pushed into another crazy place. Or eaten by a monster. Or turned into a -" Sebastian began. The coin cut him off.

There is no reason to expect the worst, you know. Looking on the bright side is how I got through thousands of years alone in this place sane.

"I can't help it." Sebastian sighed. "I always try to be realistic...that usually turns into the worst-case scenario." He slumped a little. "I just want out of here."

"I get it, man." Chester said gently. "I'm glad I found something to help my dad...but I want out soon too. I miss my mom, and my dad... he's probably wondering where I am. I visit him every day in the hospital...I can't tell time here. There's no way to."

"What if this place isn't even really in our time stream? What if we come out and we find its been several years?"

I do not know how time works in this world. I have been in this universe for so long. Sometimes it feels as if I had been transported yesterday. Sometimes the weight of time seems to rest on my copper head. The coin seemed to sigh. Well, it cooled before warming. Guess that counted as a sigh.

"Whatever. I just want out." Sebastian moaned.

"We'll get out. I know it." Chester lent some of his enthusiasm to the conversation. "We can't wander here forever. I mean, everything that has an entrance, has an exit, right?"

"I guess so." Sebastian said, looking around. The buzz of the lights was really irritating to him. It's sound was a drill in his skull.

Then, it cut out.

And with the sound went the lights.

Chester and Sebastian froze.

"Ches?" Sebastian said quietly.

"Yeah..." Chester replied. "Um...did we do something...?"

I don't think so...but...something definitely happened. The coin spoke, sounding as tense as they felt.

No one moved for several minutes.

Finally, Sebastian let out a breath. "Um...I think nothing's coming to kill us."

Chester relaxed beside him. "Yeah...I think we're ok now." He was whispering, too.

For now, we can relax. Do you have a flashlight?

"Our backpacks got left in the warehouse where we came in." Chester said. "So...no."

The coin grew warmer and suddenly began to glow, filling the area with a warm light.

Is this better?

"Much, thank you." Chester smiled and held up the coin. It was a small circle of light, but it felt comforting.

"Let's keep moving." Sebastian said, and Chester nodded. Together the two boys kept going, staying within the circle of light.

"Why did the lights go out...?" He asked, looking around. "It feels so creepy..."

As I said before... Levels of Forgetfulness. This must be the second level.

"Wait....if these are the levels of forgetfulness, does that mean...in the real world, we'll be forgotten if we're too deep?"

...I do not know. Was the only answer the coin gave to them.

Sebastian shivered. The idea of being forgotten forever...It was scary. Worse than that negative monster.

"I'm sure we'll be fine. We just can't let ourselves get stuck." Chester said. "We need to keep remembering who we are and where we came from."

I wish I had that gift...I sprung from nothing. Or, whatever I sprung from, left me alone. The coin sighed.

"Whatever you sprung from...I'm glad you did. You're the key to saving my dad." Chester said.

Suddenly there was a small thud. There, but so faint.

The two froze.

Quick! Cover my light, before you are spotted!

Chester quickly covered the coin, and they were plunged into darkness.

Another thump. Close to them.

Chester shifted, moving closer to Sebastian. He was holding his weapon aloft. Sebastian felt his own weapon dig into his hands, as he gripped it tightly.

And finally, the thing came into view.

Well...it kind of peered around the corner.

First came long, clawlike fingers, one at a time placing themselves on a wall, around the corner. And then the face.

The head itself was black, like the entity they encountered before. Except its face..it was a bright white, its eyes casting beams of light over the darkened floor.

Its face was twisted into a horrific, too-wide smile. The teeth were too sharp, the eyes too piercing. It swept its eye beams around the room, searching.

Chester and Sebastian were frozen. Once again, waves of...wrongness were coming off this smiling creature. The thing shouldn't be here.

The thing scanned the room again, coming dangerously close to where they were standing. The smile never left the thing's face.

Then, the eyebeams landed on Sebastian.

With a horrible screech the thing ran forward, revealing its full body. It looked almost like a human, running on all fours.

36

Sebastian screamed and dove to the side. Chester cursed loudly and jumped to the other side. The creature was fast, and both of them just barely avoided the creature coming at them full speed.

The claws of the creature made a screeching noise when it hit the carpeted floor. That made no sense, seeing as it was carpet. But this was the backrooms.

Sebastian looked at the creature as it focused on him. A low growl was coming from it, yet the smile never left its face.

"I think it's got a lock on me, Ches." Sebastian said, his pipe held aloft. "Maybe you can attack it from behind!"

Chester nodded, the coin in one hand and a pipe in the other. Creeping up behind the thing he unleashed a hit toward its head.

The pipe hit...and bounced off.

The thing slowly turned to Chester, eyes fixating on him.

Sebastian gasped. "What...?"

The thing lunged for Chester with a yowl. It grabbed for him with its claws.

Chester moved out of the way. "It looks like it's trying to capture us!"

"Maybe it works for Him!" Sebastian yelled back, jumping back. "It probably does...don't let it touch you!"

Wait. I have an idea. Uncover my light and shine it into the thing's eyes! The coin chose then to speak, from Chester's closed palm.

Chester whirled around and stomped his foot to get the thing's attention. When it turned to look at him, he shined the light directly into the thing's eyes.

The effect was immediate – the thing screeched in pain and covered its eyes, cringing away. It seemed to shrink under the light of the deity, as if the light repulsed it so.

"It's working!" Sebastian said as he ran behind Chester.

Chester advanced on the thing, holding the light out like a shield. It shrieked and skittered back, and then turned tail and ran, behind the corner it came out of.

Silence settled over the hallway, thick and tense.

Finally, Chester moved. Still holding the coin aloft he slowly went around the corner where the creature disappeared.

"Nothing there…" He said, looking around the corner. He seemed relieved. And concerned .

"How did it get out..that's a dead end." Sebastian said.

Because I let it. Simple as that.

The two boys whirled around. "Who -"

And they froze.

A figure was standing behind them.

A figure that radiated negative. Yet somehow it was something more. Something…more rotten and darker. Something colder.

Imagine a man. Now. Strip every single feature from his body. Face, clothes, scars, birthmarks, color, personality.

Leave in place the silhouette and make it 3 dimensional. And make it out of the darkest void available.

It was like staring into pure darkness. Pure forgetfulness.

This was Him. The man who lost Himself to the backrooms and yet fights control it. The mysterious He who controls the fallen.

It is He who is the scariest.

The lights were still off. And yet he seemed to "shine" against the darkness. If being darker than the darkness counted as that.

"You…" Sebastian stepped back. Cold fear gripped his soul, digging its icy fingers into his spine and sending pins and needles to every part of his body. Or maybe that's just a side effect of spending any time with Him in the vicinity.

"You're the one we were warned about!" Chester said, stepping back in lockstep with Sebastian. The boys moved unconsciously, as if their bodies were being repelled by whatever force He exuded.

Warned? The figure shifted. *So, there is knowledge of me around these parts…or in the world outside. Interesting…*

Do not let him know of me! The subdued but urgent plea came from the coin. He will try and absorb my power.

Sebastian nodded subtly before speaking up. "T – that's right! We were warned by…the writing on the wall!" Vague enough to be possible, not specific enough to be questioned.

So, they know how to write now. The figure seemed to sigh. Then He seemed to straighten. *No matter. Now.* He stretched out His hand. His hands seemed to lengthen, instead of Him coming closer. *I believe you're coming with me.*

Chester turned, coin clutched in his hand. "Sebastian! Run!" He yelled.

Sebastian tried to turn and run too, but it was as if his legs were molasses. "Chester...I...You need to get out of here!"

Chester moved normally. It was as if the coin in his hand protected him from the effect of the shadows.

"Sebastian!" Chester tried to reach out to him but ended up being driven away. Black hands blocked his way.

"Just go!" Sebastian yelled, his eyes now reflecting a realization that he may as well be dead.

"Seb...I can't just leave you!" Chester's voice cracked. Sebastian was rapidly being obscured by the dark hands.

"Just go! I'll be fine...I'll find you somehow!" His voice sounded watery, echoey...and yet they seemed to be imbued with resolve unheeded. "You know me. I don't give up!"

Chester nodded, but he couldn't help the tears coming to his eyes. Wiping them away, he turned and ran, the coin clutched close to him.

Behind him, he heard Him yell in frustration about losing half His prey.

He prayed Sebastian would be alright.

-

-

-

----

interlude

—   —   —

—   —

—   — — — —

He is distressed.

And here I am talking about both the boy named Chester and Him.

Sebastian...I am sorry to say I have lost mental contact. It as if a light has flickered off in my head and is refusing to come back on.

He has him now. I pray to whatever higher power, if there is one, to keep Sebastian safe. Keep his mind safe.

Chester is in deep distress.

His light keeps flickering. Scattered thoughts cross the room sometimes. Sorrow. Then anger. Then confusion. Then sorrow again.

The loss of a friend is nothing to underestimate.

I have seen humans break under the event that someone close to them passes on from this mortal life on Earth. Or that they lose contact and can't get back in touch.

Or, what's worse, is they think they've lost them. But they hold onto that forever hope that somehow, someway, someday they'll come back again. They check their phones for a message from a number collecting virtual dust. They lay awake at night thinking of all the outcomes, good and bad. They spend their days withdrawn and sullen, snapping too quickly or seeming too sad at times when they should be happy. They don't let themselves be happy, because

41

they feel like they shouldn't. They are always on the verge of tears, separated from the world by that emotional veil draped over themselves.

Well. If you've done all you could, if you were by their side until the end...then you shouldn't mourn. Rather, live as your friend would want you to live – Free and happy, but keeping their memory alive.

It's not my place to tell someone how to mourn. But those who let themselves get dragged down by something they can't control, ultimately fall into the same hole that swallowed their friend.

And who knows? Maybe someday they will get a text from that number. Maybe they will be contacted again.

You just have to have hope. And also knowledge that you did all you could. Prepare for both outcomes. It's the best advice that I could give you.

Chester...I sense your pain. I wish I could help you.

But I can't. I just can't. I will never know what it's like to lose someone that close to me.

But rest assured. I will stay by your side. I'll never abandon you. Whether it was my power that protected you or not...I'll always be here.

Now...Onto the other distress.

Him.

The dimension is churning around us, the true backrooms clashing with His will. The creatures straining at the seams of their bonds, the prison that holds them when they're not in use, but held back by some force unseen. The ooze wanting to seep but bottled up.

He gnashes his teeth in frustration. Even with one in his grip He is not satisfied. Such is the nature of nihility. It seeks to overtake everything and is never satisfied with just one more.

I fear for Chester.

Those who are grieving tend to be reckless.

Those who are grieving, when they receive news about how they could rescue their loved ones, lose rationale. They dive in headfirst, and don't care about the consequences.

I've seen it before. And the dark ends up swallowing both souls.

I will try to protect him.

On the verge of losing two.

I will not let him fall to the same dark that so many fall to.

Chester, listen to me. I am here.

Talk to me.

It's going to be ok.

Chester just kept running. For how long he didn't know. The coin clutched in his hand stayed silent. Maybe shock?

He didn't know. He didn't care.

He just lost his friend.

Finally, he sank down against a wall, out of exhaustion. The tears came, running down his face, silent sobs echoing with no noise around him.

The coin in his hand said nothing. Yet it seemed to warm, as if trying to offer comfort.

Oh God...that thing...that He...had Sebastian. Was Sebastian going to become one of those...things? A monster, unseeing or unthinking, mindless, a slave to Him?

No...that couldn't be his fate.

"Hey…" He said to the coin in his hand. His voice was choked up, thick with emotion. "Is there a way...to save Sebastian?"

The coin seemed to consider. Then -

I do not know. Likely Sebastian will be kept alive as a way to drag you in. But...Chester, you have to be prepared for the possibility -

"That I may never see him again, I get it. Why are you jumping to the worst conclusion?!" Chester snapped.

The coin fell silent.

"I'll find him. I'll find him someway...somehow…" Chester slumped against the wall; his sudden burst of angry energy spent. More tears fell from his eyes, and he leaned his head back as if he could keep them in.

Why had everything gone so wrong?

First his father, and now Sebastian…

Who else was there to lose?

His mother, his whole neighborhood, his school.

His father's chance at life?

I can tell you're upset.

"I'm sorry for snapping….I just….I…."

He didn't get father than that before breaking down.

It is ok to cry, you know. Don't feel ashamed. The coin seemed to be trying to...comfort him. In the way a thousand + year old deity could possibly comfort a modern teenager.

"Thanks." He said thickly, and wiped tears from his eyes. He opened his other hand and studied the coin. If he blinked a few times, it looked like it was glowing.

I was only able to save you from Him...I am sorry your friend was captured. The coin seemed regretful, remorseful.

"It...wasn't your fault. In that situation...you did your best."

Though Chester couldn't really say it, a deep dark part of himself blamed the deity. Blamed him for not saving Sebastian. Blamed him for it all.

That part passed him only a second later.

In any case. We should start by trying to find His lair.

"Where would that even be...?" Chester wondered. "This place is so big...and goes on forever."

...I do not know, to be honest. For all my years here, I never left that pile. But If I had to guess...He would set his lair up close to a center of this place.

"A center?"

This place is infinite. But every place has a beginning. Whatever created the backrooms...it had power. And it spread this power out to its whole...being, if I'm going to say it. But power naturally coalesces together, and little bits of power come together to form centers in the backrooms – a place where the surrounding area draws its energy to keep existing. No doubt he is using one of these centers as a base of operations, so to speak - a place he can generate this power. We have to find the specific one.*

"How will we know which is the one, and where do we even start looking? This place is infinite..."

Seeing as he can appear...we must be close to the center he took over. You'll know which one when you see it.

"I mean....yeah, I'm sure we will. probably will be dark and drippy and basically evil." Chester looked around. "...I have to find Sebastian."

I hope we can find him in time. Otherwise...

45

The deity didn't need to finish that sentence.

----

submitsubmitsubmitsubmitsubmitsubmitsubm
itsubmitsubmitsubmitsubmitsubmitsubmi
tsubmitsubmitsubmitsubmitsubmitsubmit
submitsubmitsubmitsubmitsubmitsubmits
ubmitsubmitsubmitsubmitsubmitsubmitsu
bmitsubmitsubmitsubmitsubmitsubmitsub
mitsubmitsubmitsubmitsubmitsubmitsubm
itsubmitsubmitsubmitsubmitsubmitsubmi
tsubmitsubmitsubmitsubmitsubmitsubmit
submitsubmitsubmitsubmitsubmitsubmits
ubmitsubmitsubmitsubmitsubmitsubmitsu
bmitsubmitsubmitsubmitsubmitsubmitsub
mitsubmitsubmitsubmitsubmitsubmitsubm
itsubmitsubmitsubmitsubmitsubmitsubmi
tsubmitsubmitsubmitsubmitsubmitsubmit
submitsubmitsubmitsubmit

I won't, I just won't I have too much to live for
these aren't my thoughts
are they?
You will submit you will submit you will
shut up
shut up
just SHUT UP
Do you not listen to your mind
You're not my mind shut up
Chester is out there
I'm not leaving him
not for anything
not for you

46

so you will not be broken
I WILL GO BACK TO MY FRIEND
The dark will swallow you eventually as it did me. As it has every soul who wandered back here. Why do you resist? Lost cause. Join me. Let your soul go.
A dark room. Well, sort of. Thick dark liquid dripped everywhere. Bubbles sometimes formed and burst. The backrooms wallpaper was visible, but not a lot. There were no lights. The mixture bubbled and glowed a little. It was black, and viscous.

In the center lay a boy. Black hair blending in with the surroundings. He seemed unconscious but aware. Every now and then he weakly kicked out, only for his movements to be stopped as black goop pinned him down.

Creatures circled this new prisoner. Sacrifice. Whatever you wanted to call it. But they couldn't touch him. Their Lord was at work on him.

Sometimes he would scream

Sometimes he would groan out someone's name.

Sometimes he'd arch his back.

The monsters watched silently, empty eyes taking in what they once were.

Human.

Pain feeling.

Existing.

They stewed. They silently murmured. Some reached out, only to be slapped back by the black goopy tendrils.

H e i s m i n e

And they understood and drew back

They would get the remains.

Once He was done…

47

Chester walked more.
What else was there to say?
Not all parts of a story are glamorous.

The domain of the unknowns spans a lot of space.
Even in the infinite backrooms, it will take over.
Rot knows no bounds.
And so, it spread, as He did.
Carpet became saturated, walls became slick.
Goo covered everything.
Molasses, trapping everything that flies into it.
Sebastian one of those flies
He lay there still.
Fighting.
Why he fought no one knew.
The monsters murmured to each other in their silent language. Why someone would bother fighting such an overwhelming dark.
Meanwhile, He gnashed his teeth.

Why won't you SUBMIT?
You would never understand.
My friend keeps me going

He will die like the rest
Chester's too strong.

Is he? Or is he just putting up a facade?
Shut up.

For an instant I saw into his head, you know. And he's breaking. School. His father. He doesn't know who he is or who he wants to be. Bullied for wearing pink. Jokes about his father. His mother always on the verge of a breakdown. Never having enough money. Wanting to be there all the

48

time but never seeming to be able to. No matter what, never being enough, even if he were to give his soul to the very things that plague his friends.

I SAID SHUT UP!

Do not yell at me. This is his mind. Sometimes he gets angry at you, you know. Sometimes he's resentful of what you have. Wishes he had what you did. Sometimes he wants to yell at you. Coveting what you have – stable parents. Income that does not fluctuate. A good life.

JUST…JUST GO AWAY!

A laugh.

Then more silence, and more pain.

He wouldn't let go…he couldn't. He fought it with all his might.

He would keep his mind.

He had to.

He would never leave his best friend alone. No matter what he thought of him.

Meanwhile the turmoil continued in the dimension.

The black ooze bubbled and tried to take over. The dimension pushed back, attempting to contain the wound that was Him.

Was the buzzing getting louder?

Chester couldn't tell. It seemed to fluctuate – soft and then loud.

All he knew was that this place was frustrating him.

His emotions were already a wreck, and the fact that this endless maze of stupid yellow was still not giving him any direction was ticking him off endlessly.

Wasn't this dimension supposed to be helping him? If the dimension wanted him to get rid of the mysterious He, then why wasn't it making this any easier?!

Chester clenched his fist, feeling the nails dig into his palm. "Why..." He murmured to himself. Then, louder. "WHY?"

Chester, calm down! We will be heard! The coin urged.

"Sorry. I just...this place is supposed to be helping us. Why is it not...?"

Perhaps...it is. Look at the ground you're standing on.

Chester looked down and made an interesting observation – There seemed to be a difference – the carpet was darker here. And did it...squish under his feet?

He looked at the walls. Was it just him, or was there black spots here?

The center tried to hide itself. Even the Backrooms itself has limited control over this space now. It's doing its best...and you are too. Don't give up.

Chester swallowed nervously and nodded, clutching the coin for comfort. He stepped forward and suddenly -

```
 tiltingtiltingtiltingtiltingtilting
suddenly
the world rightened
And Chester found himself in the Center.
His Center.
Black ooze everywhere
It smelled like...
Decay but if decay was sweet and sour at
the same time
 The smell of dead dreams is a scent that
is hard to place.
 And the noises...
```

Chester coughed in the sickly sweet air. The scent was too thick…
He hated this. It was too much, all at once.
And it felt like the black muck was sucking him down.
He had to move. Or else it really would suck him down.
Chester lifted his leg from the sucking black muck. Then the other. It made a sucking sound, like wet mud trying to drag him down. He struggled out of the puddle and looked around more.
It was so dark here.
And he could hear them.
The things, moving in the darkness.
They murmured and shifted, in a language he could not understand.
They watched him with wide, white eyes. Moving and shifting around him. Reaching out only to quickly draw back, repelled from him by the force of the deity.
If it wasn't for the coin, he was sure he would be dead. Or worse.
He had to find his friend.
We must hurry, Chester. Your friend is somewhere here, and even I cannot keep Him out entirely.
"I know. Let's just focus on moving forward." Ignoring the slurry that pooled around his ankles, he did his best to move forward.
It was slow going, the muck sucked and bubbled around his feet. The things around him couldn't touch him, but they tried. Reaching out with goopy hands, dripping black sludge. Whispers of an unknown origin emanated from...somewhere. He couldn't tell.
He just needed to keep moving.

Just keep going. Find his friend.

He comes for you, you know.
What?
He is in my lair now. Coming to find you.
No...I can't let him get hurt
Too late now, Sebastian.
You know my name?
Of course I do. I've accessed your mind. If you think you can keep me out, boy, you're very wrong.
Around the dormant boy the black ooze shifted. Wrapping around him like a blanket. The boy struggled, but this time the ooze didn't give him a choice, wrapping him entirely in muck. The muck shaped into a being, this one different than the others. Perhaps because it had a living core, one that still remembered humanity.

It was...lopsided. Sludgy. Not fully formed. Vaguely oval shaped eyes blinked to life and flickered on and off. Two long limbs formed, reaching to the ground and running into the muck. A hunched back formed.

The thing that was powered by Sebastian looked around. It tested its movements. Then it looked up at its creator.

Good. Very good. He looked the creature over. Though he was slightly dissatisfied by the apparent...incompleteness of the creature, it would work for his purpose, nonetheless.

Go. Find him and bring him here - so I may see the despair in his eyes as he is destroyed by his best friend.
The creature tilted his head in acknowledgment and limped off. Heading

52

toward Chester – or where he thought he was.

Meanwhile Chester was still wandering. He struggled through the goop that sucked at his knees now, finding it hard and tricky to move through, like molasses. Yet the comforting warmth of the deity coin in his hand seemed to loosen it, for a moment, and he kept moving forward.

Not just for himself.

For his father.

For Sebastian.

What else can you do, when you're in that situation?

Nowhere else to go, struggling in muck, afraid for everyone you care for?

There are some who would give up. Curl up and let the muck take them, sink down in their own despair.

And yet…

And yet…

There are those who continue on. Those who struggle through those dark times no matter how bleak it may seem, those who carry a backbreaking load and still manage to go forward, one stumbling step at a time.

And it's those people who, in the darkest of times, will shine the brightest.

Chester was one of those. And he kept slogging through the muck – intent on keeping it up.

Until he heard the sound of a monster.

Chester tensed up. He felt the coin heat up in his hand.

And then the monster came around the corner.

The lopsided amalgamation that used Sebastian as a battery.

53

Chester somehow knew. That this was his best friend – or, rather, the thing that was holding his best friend captive.

Why? He didn't know. Perhaps it was the eyes – seeming to be pleading for help, despite its body language. Perhaps how it looked half – formed, as if fighting itself. Or maybe it was just one of those things best friends knew.

However he knew, he realized his best friend was in more trouble than originally realized.

"Sebastian!"

The creature gave no acknowledgement to that name. It limped over to Chester, who was still trying to pull himself out of the muck and wrapped its two slimy appendages around him. Chester struggled and the coin, in alarm, became a red – hot coal in his hand. He nearly dropped it because of the pain, but sheer survival instinct told him to hang onto that no matter what. So he did.

The monster didn't hurt him. At least, not now. Instead, holding Chester firmly in its goopy grip, it began walking. It seemed to know where it was going – turning this way and that way. Chester knew that it was taking him to...Him. His center.

The thought excited him and terrified him. He had access to His base now. But on the other hand...he could very well die here and no one would know what became of him.

Chester could feel the muck against his skin. It seemed alive in ways muck should not be – sliding around his body and skin, as if feeling what Chester was. And looking for ways to suffocate him.

It seemed forever until they reached the Center. And Chester had to stifle a gasp.

It looked like any other infected room in the backrooms. Only…way, way bigger.

This room seemed to extend into forever. Black goo covered everything – the walls, the ceiling, even the broken light fixtures that weakly buzzed with one last bit of charge dripped with black stuff. Creatures milled around, though swiveled their heads to see the newcomers arrive. Whispery voices picked up as they began to chatter amongst themselves, in the language of the forgotten.

In the middle sat a throne – like mass, made out of hardened goo that shone a little in the dim light. And reclining on the throne was Him.

Glad to see you're back, Chester. If He could grin there would be a big one plastered on his face right now.

Chester looked at him coolly, trying to portray confidence even though he was terrified. "Can't really say the same about you." His tone was nonchalant, but there was the slightest tremble in his voice.

The He let out a small chuckle. It seemed to reverberate around the room. He stood up and walked over to Chester. He walked over the muck effortlessly, as if he was walking on flat ground. Chester wondered how he was doing that.

I see your reunion with your friend went well. He said in a teasing tone. Well, as teasing as one could get telepathically.

Chester didn't dignify that with a response. He just set his lips in a line and glared at Him.

I admit, you two were the first to give me a hard time back here. To think those that know nothing of the forgotten nearly threw a wrench in my plans... No matter. Not now. He shook his head. *I offer you a choice. Join me willingly, join your friend, and I will have no further reason to inflict pain upon you. But refuse, and I will have your friend break your neck.*

"I will never join you. And I know that Sebastian would never follow that order. No matter what you did to him...He's still in there somewhere. Fighting."

Also. You forget one thing. The creatures cannot touch -

Deity, I see that you are blind. The creature with a living battery can still touch him.

Chester's heart leapt into his throat. Living battery? Sebastian was alive.

I see you finally decide to acknowledge my existence. Took you long enough – especially seeing as I can resist your creatures and even your influence.

Shut up. Your religion is dead - and has been for so long. You ended up here along with the rest of the forgotten - it is only because of these two children you have any semblance of power.

And it's because of these children I have another chance. If I may, they have already proved to be much more powerful than you ever were.

That's hilarious. They're both weak - One, I even managed to turn into my slave. Face it. Your time is up, and so is theirs.

Now you're the one being hilarious. If the coin could laugh it would. These boys are stronger than you realize. Sure, they're human. They have human problems and human flaws.

56

But then again, who doesn't have flaws? You were once human, I'm sure you remember you had flaws.

And I surpassed my humanity and erased the weak flaws I had! He seemed visibly agitated, and though he had no face the way he clenched his fist was definitely an indication on how he was feeling.

Humans will be humans. Even if they become immortal. I have flaws and I am immortal. No living being is without flaws – even gods make mistakes.

Shut your mouth. When these boys are gone, you'll fade back into oblivion. Back into just a metal coin with barely a conscious and no power. And then I'll deal with you, because I'll have more power.

The coin said nothing. But in Chester's hand it seemed to pulse with warmth – fear? Or defiance? He didn't know.

Now. Back to you, Chester. Yes, I know your name - your friend's mind opened easily to me once I changed him. You must decide now. Join me willingly, or else I will have your friend be the one to end you.

"I will never join you. And I know Seb will never, ever kill me."

Are you sure? I was able to turn him into a creature. Or did you already forget the thing holding you now is your friend?

Or rather, would be, if it was complete. Chester, I know your senses aren't as developed, but I can sense something living inside this creature. Your friend lives, and your friend is fighting. Also, I noticed this Sebastian – creature is half formed, as if you still -

S/H_U_T/ _U_P/!~

He slammed his fist down on the throne. A tremor seemed to go through the room – the creatures swayed and shifted uneasily. Chester felt some kind of electrical zing go through him as if he had received a minor shock. The Sebastian – creature let out a quiet noise of...something. Even the coin in Chester's hand went cool for a moment.

Dead silence after that. Then He spoke again.

You are most vexing, deity. Perhaps I will absorb your power myself. Then he looked back at Chester.

The time has come. Choose, boy.

•••

  •••

    •••

  •••

I'm here
I'm here
I'm not you
I was never you
I am the new you, Sebastian.
I reject you.
You are not me.
      ACCEPT ME
Speaking louder won't make me

k
    I
        L
           L
              H
                  I
                      M

I can't, I won't -

D O I T

I SAID I WOULD NOT

KILL HIM

NOW

I don't want to.

You will obey me

I will not!

Your

friend

will

die. You
are
already
dead.
Give in
to me
already.

A sound in the darkness.
A light. Chester saying "no."
He gave the order to the Sebastian
creature.
And for a split second, Sebastian's mind –
vision went dark–
before a supernova.

I AM

STILL

HERE. I

WILL

NOT GIVE IN.

Chester didn't hear any of these words. But he did feel the tremor that ran through the body of the behemoth that held him, and then felt himself being dropped. He watched as its eyes flickered out and it seemed to melt before his very eyes -
And when it cleared...
Sebastian was lying on the floor in front of him. Still slightly covered in the black goo, but...hey.
His chest was moving.
He was breathing.
He was alive.
Nothing moved for ten seconds. Possibly longer. Chester stared at Sebastian. The Coin in his hand said nothing but warmed up. The monsters' whispering had ceased.
And He was frozen in the seat.
Never had someone defied him so. Never had a soul struggled so hard it was let go.
He stood up.

KILL

THEM

ALL!

The tension was broken. The goopy creatures
surged forward, with a combined scream of
hate, drawn from their master.
The coin in Chester's hand heated up, as if
ready for conflict.
And then…

Another surge.
But this one unfamiliar.

THAT IS

A surge of power.
The lights, previously dead, violently buzzed to life with a sound so loud it pierced through everything. Some light bulbs popped because of the ferocity. The creatures howled in pain at the sudden bright light, some even melting away.
And He writhed as well, exposed to the light and...something else.

I thought you had been vanquished!

Well, you thought very wrong, then – I was never vanquished! I cannot be, or else this realm would have ceased to exist long ago. I am this very room you're in, you just covered it up enough to where I could not take it back. And yet these two boys, and this deity – they helped me do what I could not on my own. Break free of you.

I will not...I will not die here! I can't...not after all I have done –

You cannot escape your fate. I am the judge, jury, and executioner of this realm, and I have watched you turn this sacred final resting place for the forgotten into an insidious, evil realm. I have listened to you talk to yourself about taking over all the realms, turning it into a hellscape. And for what? You say you want to see what happens when all of humanity is forgotten. Your twisted curiosity has led to the death of innocents. You have perverted this land.

You

must

PERISH

No!

His writhing form broke apart and reformed. As if he was being taken apart but putting himself back together despite it.

The boys huddled together. The surviving creatures around them howled with their master and melted away. Some lasted longer than the others, but all in all they all melted back into the goo from whence they came.

The struggle continued. The air around them seemed to buzz with electricity, or some energy that didn't have any other word. All the boys knew was that they were watching a battle far beyond their mortal comprehension.

In fact, the only reason they weren't being vaporized was the protection of the coin deity – it was casting an invisible wall to protect them.

It took a long time to the humans

67

Yet it was over in only an instant.
The only reason He had survived for so
long was because He tried so hard to be
forgotten at the beginning, He had been.
And He had grown because of it. But as He
grew, so did his ambitions.
And just like a white blood cell finds an
infection and destroys it, the deity of the
backrooms found Him.
Inevitably, it was His fate to be utterly
forgotten.
Destroyed forever.
A flash of light…
All encompassing.
And then…

They were back.

The first thing the two felt was a cold floor. Not carpet. Actual floor.

Chester was up first. He groaned and shifted, sitting up. His eyes slowly began to adjust to the low light of the...

Warehouse.

Not the backrooms.

A Warehouse.

They were out. Somehow.

He saw Sebastian lying close to the backpacks. The ones they'd dropped when they first came in.

He went to stand up when he felt something in his hand.

The coin.

Chester stared at it. Then he began to laugh. Not the laugh of a crazy person, no.

The laugh of triumph. He had a way to save his father.

"Why are you laughing...?" Sebastian shifted. He groaned as he sat up. There was no trace of the black goo on him. Nothing to suggest he had been held captive by an otherworldly monster.

"Seb. The coin... it's here. It's real. We can save my father..."

Sebastian smiled and pushed himself up, then winced. "Ah god...I feel like I've been run over by something." He slowly pushed himself up and sat against a crate.

Then something occurred to them.

"How long have we been gone?" Said Sebastian.

"...I don't know..." Chester reached for his backpack. He fished around. If the backpacks had been untouched...there! His phone, resting at the bottom. He pulled it out, thankful. It still had about half charge – more or less how he left it.

"If we went into the backrooms about October 1st..." He opened his phone and then went absolutely still.

"...Ches?" Sebastian said, looking up worried.

"...It's October 2nd. Nearly noon." Chester seemed awed.

"...It felt like we were in there forever! How did not even a day pass..."

Time works differently in different dimensions.

The boys jumped and Chester looked down at his coin again. "...You can still talk here?"

Much better, actually. I feel clearer. Now that I am out of there… I can think. I feel my power returning.

"…What happened back there?" Sebastian said quietly. "…I remember a flash of light. He was fighting with the backrooms itself it seemed...but then…"

… I felt it too. An ancient power...something older than even me. The deity that created the backrooms… was older than time itself. Perhaps the forgotten are.

"…I feel like we won. We won, didn't we?" Sebastian said, smiling hopefully.

We did. I felt it as we were transported out. The deity let us go, for we had saved it. I felt it.

"I mean, you're the one with god senses. Gotta trust you." Chester said. "…So, what now?"

I have a promise to keep. It's time to save your father.

And Chester's eyes finally lit up with true light.

Things changed after that.

The coin deity kept his promise and more. Chester's father made a miraculous recovery from his sickness. The doctors were astounded.

And so was his mom and dad.

Chester told his mom and dad about the coin. He didn't tell them about the backrooms. He would probably have gotten in trouble for going to an abandoned warehouse.

And they started a new religion. The only problem was that the coin deity had no name.

So they asked it to choose what it wanted to be called.

It chose Omni. For it meant all, and that is who the deity served. Everyone.

Sebastian chose to join that religion, because his parents didn't really care what he did. And he managed to get them signed up. When they heard Omni talk they were sold.

It seems like an anti - climactic ending to the story right? Everyone ending up happy and stuff.

70

Well sometimes life ends up that way, and it's good it does. Everyone deserves happiness at some point. A life without happiness is just a life survived. Not lived.

The backrooms itself still survive to this day. No more goopy creatures roam the halls. No more Him.

Just a resting place for the forgotten.

And I hope it stays that way for a long, long time.

Olivia Hufford is a Cincinnati teenager who lives in the Green Township area. She attends Walnut Hills High School. She loves writing and began writing at a young age, starting with fanfiction and moving on to original stories as she got older. Her favorites are horror and science fiction/fantasy stories. She spends most of her time reading or daydreaming about what worlds lie beyond our galaxy and what dimensions lie beyond our perception.